The Wall and the Wild

CHRISTINA DENDY

KATIE REWSE

Lantana

At the end of Ironbark Way, the town of Stone Hollow edges against the WILD.

There, Ana turns a patch of bare earth. Seed by seed, drop by drop, Ana grows a garden. Lovely, tidy, and thick with life.

"Perfect," she says.

She wants to keep it that way, so—
Ana picks out the most perfect-seeming seeds.
"Not too big. Not too small. No breaks. No bruises."

The rest she throws into the untidy WILD.

"YOU, stay out THERE."

Ana lines the boundary between her orderly patch and the disorderly WILD.

Ana's garden grows.

And **grows.**

And **grows.**

Leafy trees, tasty fruits and vegetables, sweet-smelling flowers.

Birds, bees, and butterflies hum. Critters, some with four legs,
some with more, nibble. People stop to look.

Yes, Ana grows a WONDROUS garden, but—

"What's this?" she asks. "I didn't plant you."
Ana plucks and pitches the unfamiliar sprout.
Then she picks through her seeds.

"Too dull. Too round.
Too thin. Too tough."

More fly into the grubby WILD.

"YOU, stay out THERE."

Ana builds her boundary a little higher.

Ana's garden grows.

And **grows.**

Less leafy, less tasty, less sweet-smelling.

Fewer birds, bees, and butterflies hum. Fewer critters nibble. Fewer people visit.

Ana trims and thins, and pinches and prunes, but—
"More of you?" she asks. "Not here, you don't."

Ana tugs and tosses the unwanted shoots,
then picks through her seeds.

"Too bright.

Too thick.

Too flat.

Too soft."

"YOU. STAY. OUT. THERE."

Most soar into the messy WILD.

Ana builds the boundary as high as she can—

Until she has a **MIGHTY WALL.**

Ana's garden grows.

Thinning leaves, dull blooms, pinched fruits.

Birds, bees, and butterflies hum away.
Critters scamper and scurry to find tastier nibbles.

No one stops.

Ana waters and feeds her plants, but—
"Bracken and brush!" she fumes. "WHAT is going on?"

Ana surveys the constellation of uninvited leaves, grass, and vines.
They reach over, through, and under the wall, while shadows
creep across the fading flowers of her garden.

On the other side, voices babble, footsteps patter,
and sunlight beams.

Ana marches to the wall.
She climbs up ᵁᴾ up and sees—

"WOW."

The seeds Ana threw away have grown.
Deep but bright, tangled but rich, strange
but wonderful. "Perfect," she says.

She wants to keep it that way, so—
Ana climbs down the wall.

And pulls loose a stone.

At the end of Ironbark Way, the town of
Stone Hollow edges against the wild.

There, Ana and her friends tend the rich earth.
Seed by seed, drop by drop, a garden and a
wilderness grow. Together.

DID YOU KNOW ... ?

Scientists *know* that well over a million species of life exist on Earth. They *think* that more than 8 million species exist. A species is a group that shares certain traits. So far, scientists have identified about 1 million animal species, including humans. Most—around 950,000—are insects, like ants, bees, and butterflies. There are also around 300,000 species of plants.

Many different species share areas of land and water. These areas and the species that live in them are called ecosystems. An ecosystem can be large, like an ocean, or small, like a garden. Ecosystems are communities. Everything that lives in them affects everything else.

Ecosystems need many species to do well. That's because living things rely on each other for food and other necessities. A garden ecosystem like Ana's needs many types of plants to grow, as well as the help of insects and other animals. It also needs sunlight, soil, and fresh water.

Seeds like the ones Ana plants come in many shapes, sizes, and textures. They get bruises and scratches just like you do. They still grow. Seeds don't need to look the same or "perfect" to grow into perfectly beautiful, healthy plants.

Your community is an ecosystem, too! It needs different people to help it grow. The people in your ecosystem don't have to look, act, believe, or be the same to create a beautiful, healthy place.

VARIETY MAKES FOR A BRIGHT, RICH, WONDROUS GARDEN!

For Ori, Nova and Quinn, my own wild and wondrous
sprouts, and Geoff, my most beloved gardener
– *CHRISTINA*

For Zara and Jesse
– *KATIE*

First published in the United Kingdom in 2021 by Lantana Publishing Ltd.
www.lantanapublishing.com | info@lantanapublishing.com

American edition published in 2021 by Lantana Publishing Ltd., UK.

Text © Christina Dendy, 2021
Illustration © Katie Rewse, 2021

Distributed in the United States and Canada by Lerner Publishing Group, Inc.
241 First Avenue North, Minneapolis, MN 55401 U.S.A.
For reading levels and more information, look for this title at www.lernerbooks.com
Cataloging-in-Publication Data Available.

Hardback ISBN: 978-1-913747-43-5
eBook PDF: 978-1-913747-44-2
ePub3: 978-1-913747-45-9

Printed and bound in China
Original artwork created using mixed media, completed digitally